MW01170019

The Playboy's Pretend Fiancée
A Fortuna, Texas Novella

Rochelle Bradley

The Playboy's Pretend Fiancée was originally released in *Beauty for Ashes: Authors & Dancers Against Cancer Anthology* published July 27, 2020 benefiting DAC.

EPIC

DREAMS

PUBLISHING, LLC

Published by Epic Dreams Publishing, LLC
EpicDreamsPublishing.com

Visit: RochelleBradley.com

ISBN 978-1-947561-15-1

ACKNOWLEDGMENTS

Thanks to my great beta team: Brandy G, Laura B, Aliya Dalrae, Dawn Paul, CJ Baty, and Jessica Luna. Y'all help make me a better writer.

Kudos to my friends who were brave enough to help me keep my sanity through quarantine. You are the best!

Special thanks to Sharon for putting up with my scatterbrained Zoom calls. I appreciate your friendship and all the suggestions.

DEDICATION

For Nik.

A NOTE FROM ROCHELLE

Dear Reader,

Welcome to Fortuna, Texas where the men read romance. This sweet Fortuna novella is Sawyer and Stephanie's story. You can read this story as a standalone, but both characters are introduced in The Double D Ranch. Sawyer is quite the player and has moments in all the full-length novels.

If you'd like more of Sawyer and Stephanie's backstory, feel free to read the other Fortuna books.

Thank you and happy reading!

~Rochelle

CHAPTER ONE
Stephanie

HIDDEN AMONG THE HEDGE SHADOWS, Stephanie Malone waited for her aunt. Laughter from the manor house reminded her she hadn't been invited to the gala. Unaccustomed to high heels, she shifted in the grass, keeping the spikes from sinking into the soft earth.

"There you are," Amber hissed. She had straightened her wavy, blonde bob for the shindig. "Why are you skulking in the bushes like a thief?"

Stephanie stopped herself from rolling her eyes and blew out a sigh. "Maybe because we shouldn't be here."

"It's the best chance I have to speak to Gillian Nocker. You know how much I want a part in the play," Amber said, narrowing her gaze to study a couple ringing the doorbell. "Besides, I know you want to see inside the house."

Stephanie grinned, her silence revealing the truth. She scanned the windows, watching the smiling people converse.

"Come on." Amber tugged Stephanie's elbow.

"I don't know about this," Stephanie said, following Amber.

1

"What's the worst that can happen?" Amber threw a wry grin over her shoulder as she stepped onto the porch.

"Well, we could get arrested for trespassing, for one," Stephanie grumbled, hugging herself.

"You worry too much," Amber said. "It'll be fun."

"You look like you belong, but…" Stephanie glanced at her knee-length blue dress.

Ignoring the comment, Amber took Stephanie's elbow and tugged again. "You look classy."

"I'd only wear a dress to help you," Stephanie said.

"I know." Amber giggled. "Your legs deserve freedom. Maybe you'll dance with that gorgeous playboy tonight."

Stephanie froze, jerking Amber to a stop. "No way. He knows he's hot and flirts with everyone. I will not be a notch on his bedpost."

Amber gazed into her eyes as Stephanie tried to swallow a lump in her throat.

They walked to the door, following another couple. The man in a black suit jacket pushed the doorbell. The beveled glass sparkled in the light as the wide door swung open.

"Welcome," a woman greeted. "Your hosts are in the ballroom. Follow me." She turned and led the group down the hallway.

The foyer boasted a sweeping stairwell that divided into two, each leading to its own wing. The tall ceiling held simple yet thick crown molding. Amber cleared her throat, catching Stephanie's attention, and she hurried to catch up.

"I knew you'd love the house," Amber whispered.

"It's so grand," Stephanie breathed, passing a lit niche filled with crystal.

Murmuring partygoers gathered in the hall as they entered the room. "Here you are," the woman announced. "Enjoy your evening."

The couple waved to friends and then disappeared into the crowd. Amber and Stephanie stood next to the wall, observing.

After a minute Amber brightened. "There she is." She smiled and pointed to an elderly woman.

"Are you sure you want to approach her here?" Stephanie cautioned.

Amber rolled her eyes. "I didn't put on pantyhose for nothing." She inhaled deeply and snatched a glass of pink liquid from a tray of a passing server.

"May I have one," Stephanie asked the man, who frowned after her aunt.

"Yes, miss," he said, holding the tray for her.

Stephanie picked a glass, then watched her aunt schmooze with the play director from the neighboring town. Amber had a beautiful voice, but the underhanded attempt to gain the Nockerville resident's attention might come back to haunt them both.

Stephanie moved to the other side of the room, slowing beside Seymour Hickey when he said, "The treasure." He held a highball glass filled with golden liquid. His gray, nearly bald head caught the light as he tipped his head with a twinkle in his eye.

Stephanie turned, concealing her gasp. Discovering the Cummings' treasure had been a story kids had reenacted while playing. As an adult, she'd put it aside as a myth.

"How about you, little missy?" Seymour asked, tapping on her arm.

"Excuse me?" Stephanie responded nervously. The patriarch of the manor could throw her out.

But he smiled. "What have you heard about the Cummings'

treasure?"

Stephanie's mouth flopped open, and she shook her head.

"Come now," Seymour said, crinkling his eyes, his brows forming one white line.

"Um. As a kid, I heard it was a stagecoach heist, but I also heard it could have been a train robbery."

"Did you know about the curse?" Seymour asked.

She rubbed her head. "I don't recall anything regarding a curse."

"I do," a velvety masculine voice responded from behind her. "We're cursed to never find the dang thing."

Stephanie stiffened, refusing to turn, and sipped her wine.

"Oh, tell me," Morgan Topp said to Seymour. Morgan was a Fortuna social worker and an acquaintance of Stephanie's mother. Stephanie nodded in greeting.

She glanced around, finding double doors open toward the outside. Stephanie edged toward the doors, then exited onto the patio. A few bistro tables held revelers sampling hors d'oeuvres. She once again hid in a shadow, watching her aunt fling her hands around as she talked. Gillian Nocker held a smile.

"Maybe Aunt Amber will get lucky after all," Stephanie murmured with a smile.

"Who's getting lucky?" More than curiosity, the warm, buttery words floated to her with an offer, making her knees weak. Stephanie almost dropped her glass. She covered her thumping heart, cursing her imagination.

"Sorry," he said, stepping nearer. "I seem to have that effect on all the ladies." He offered his hand. "Sawyer Hickey."

Everyone in Fortuna knew bloody well who the Hickeys were. Stephanie frowned until she stared into his eyes, eyes that twinkled with friendliness through sinfully long lashes. She couldn't help her lips as they transformed into a grin. She took his large hand.

"Stephanie Malone. My aunt Amber and I have crashed your party," she admitted.

"Oh really," he said, his eyes narrowing before crinkling as he chuckled. "I won't tell my aunt Wanda if you won't."

Laughter burst from the room, and Sawyer glanced up. "Actually, I'm glad you're here. I think you're the only person close to my age."

Stephanie studied the party attenders. "I suppose you're right. Wow."

"A few of the caterers are younger, but…" He shrugged.

"I guess I need to stay away from your aunt, since she'll know I wasn't invited." Stephanie sidestepped toward the ballroom and out of Sawyer's space, finding Amber beside a grand piano handing sheet music to the director. The woman cracked her knuckles. Amber sipped from a glass of iced water.

"Looks like a singalong," Stephanie muttered.

"Groovy," Sawyer said, shadowing her again.

His breath caused shivers to run down her spine. Stephanie found it hard to breathe even though she stood outside.

"Sawyer," a feminine voice drifted from somewhere on the patio.

"Uh oh. It's my aunt. Move inside the room, behind the wall where she can't see you."

Stephanie nodded and advanced into the room. She waved at Amber but listened to Sawyer's conversation.

"Auntie Wanda, did I tell you what a picture you are in pink?" he gushed.

Wanda twittered. "Thank you." After a moment, she asked,

"Who was that young woman?"

Stephanie peeked around the wall. Sawyer had hugged a tiny lady with short snow-white hair. He glanced up and winked at Stephanie. She heated and retreated out of sight.

"Oh, you noticed her?" he asked slyly.

"I saw you noticed her too."

"Yes, ma'am. Her dress caught my eye. It's the color of bluebonnets."

Stephanie glanced down at her dress and smiled. Sawyer had picked the exact reason she'd purchased the dress.

"That did not answer my question, young man."

"She's the niece of one of your friends. I hope you don't mind she tagged along."

Once more Stephanie sneaked a peek at Sawyer. He held his aunt's hands and grinned affectionately down at her. Warmed by Sawyer's relationship with his aunt, Stephanie smiled at hers. Amber belted out the finale of the song. The director nodded. Their covert mission was on the brink of success.

"I'm glad she's here. We're going to go treasure hunting," Sawyer said.

"Oh, that stupid treasure," Wanda grumbled.

"Auntie," Sawyer said.

"Fine. Don't get into any trouble."

Sawyer laughed, and his aunt joined him.

Stephanie jumped when he touched her hand. He laced his fingers with hers, sending a jolt up her arm. "Come on."

She glanced helplessly toward her singing aunt, who belted out a show tune. Stephanie gave up resisting and let him sweep her away.

"Where are we going?" she asked.

"Treasure hunting," Sawyer replied, turning down a narrow

passage. It opened into a two-story library. One wall was floor-to-ceiling windows, another was shelves and shelves of books.

"Wow," Stephanie whispered. Her finger skimmed the spines of the closest shelf. The gold-embossed, leather-bound covers appeared ancient.

Near the window, a cast iron staircase spiraled to a second-floor ledge. The ledge wrapped around to the open balcony overlooking the library.

Sawyer plopped into a burgundy leather chair with claw and ball feet and rubbed his hands. "I like this room."

"Me too," Stephanie replied, feeling behind her for the matching chair.

Recessed lights bathed the room with a soft glow, accentuating the enormous fireplace gracing the other wall. Tiles in fall colors surrounded the firebox in stark contrast to the white marble mantle.

"So, this is the treasure," Stephanie breathed, studying the huge hunting picture that hung above the fireplace.

Sawyer chuckled, and Stephanie glanced at him. He ran his fingers through his hair and grinned as she followed the motion.

"No, but it's rumored to have something to do with this room," he said, rubbing his chin.

"Don't you know?" she asked, inspecting the rows of books again.

"Not really."

Stephanie jumped to her feet with her hands on her hips and eyeballed him. "This is your house and your family. Surely, you've got to know something."

Sawyer rose abruptly, matching her stance and leaning into her space. "I've already told you the something. It has to do with this room. And don't call me Shirley."

"I, uh?" Stephanie stepped backward. She shook her head and laughed.

"My dad said this room is the key to the treasure." Sawyer strode to the books and waved. "I think a clue has to be in a book, but which one?"

Stephanie tilted her head, reading the titles. She worked her way down the row. A book caught her eye about seven feet up.

"I might have found something," she said, taking the cast iron stairs. Her shoes clanged as she circled until she was close to the book.

"What is it?" Sawyer asked from below her.

"*Treasure Island.*" She struggled to rein in her excitement as she peered down into his shining eyes.

"Awesome." He smirked. "Why didn't I think of that before?"

"A book about a treasure hiding a clue about another treasure..." Stephanie shrugged. She stretched her hand toward the book. It was just out of reach. Determined, she leaned against the rail and reached further.

"I wouldn't—" Sawyer started.

The iron rail gave way at the seam. Stephanie screamed as she plummeted through the air—right into Sawyer's muscular arms.

CHAPTER TWO

Sawyer

FIVE YEARS LATER...

Sawyer stuck a hand in the warm sudsy water and retrieved a plate. It seemed none of the other ranch hands knew how to wash dishes. He'd had to soak the pile before he filled the dishwasher.

Gimme Malone and Chappy Pitts watched a movie behind him. Sawyer tried to tune out their banter, listening to the soundtrack of *Dirty Dancing*.

"I can dance like that," Gimme declared.

"Bull," Chappy replied.

"Just watch me," Gimme said.

Sawyer turned with a smirk. Gimme swung his hips and mimicked the actors on the screen. Loading the last dish, Sawyer couldn't contain his laughter.

"What?" Gimme demanded with his hands on his hips.

"Nothing." Sawyer dropped onto the sofa next to Chappy. He motioned to Gimme. "Continue."

Gimme turned around and twerked, earning more laughter.

He scowled. "I'll have you know, the ladies like my dancing."

"Which ladies?" Sawyer asked.

"His sisters." Chappy sniggered, elbowing Sawyer.

"Hey, leave my sisters alone," Gimme growled.

Chappy punched the air with his finger. "When you grow up in a house full of girls, you know a thing or two about the ladies," he said, copying Gimme's tone.

The younger man frowned. "Well, it's true." Gimme stared out the window.

"So which sister taught you to dirty dance?" Chappy asked.

"Stephanie?" Sawyer was sure the Fortuna Savings and Loan bank manager had never danced dirty. The memory of her in his arms flashed in his mind's eye. With her soft warmth pressed against him, he had gazed mesmerized when her kiss-swollen lips parted in a sigh.

Gimme glowered out the window with his arms crossed. Chappy and Sawyer shared a look and a grin.

"The lawyer is here and going to Mr. Davidson's house," Gimme finally said.

Chappy and Sawyer gathered at the window beside Gimme. Warren Teed clambered up the steps onto the Big Deal Ranch house's wide porch.

"That suit looks expensive." Chappy rubbed his hay-colored hair.

"And hot," Gimme added.

"Cool Mercedes." Chappy pointed to the silver sedan.

"He's a lawyer. Must be nice to be made of money. Huh, Sawyer?" Gimme glanced at him, but Sawyer ignored the prod, and instead, focused on Brad Davidson greeting Warren with a handshake. Brad nodded and motioned toward the bunkhouse.

"They're coming over here," Gimme said, stating the

obvious.

Chappy and Sawyer shared a glance, and Chappy rolled his eyes.

"Maybe you should throw your trash away?" Sawyer suggested.

Gimme grabbed the empty microwave popcorn bag and soda can. He scurried to tidy up as Brad swung open the door.

Warren met Sawyer's gaze and nodded.

"Howdy," Brad greeted. He scrutinized the room, landing on the paused movie. "Sorry to interrupt your downtime, but we have a visitor." Brad introduced his ranch hands to Warren.

"Welcome." Chappy stuck out his oversized mitt.

"Sawyer, if I may have a word...?" Warren started.

"Okay." Sawyer glanced at the other men.

Brad sauntered toward the back and opened the door to the bunk room. "Let's give them some privacy." Gimme and Chappy silently shadowed Brad like sad puppies. With a click, the door latched, leaving an awkward silence.

Warren cleared his throat. "Let's sit." He moved to the small round table and pulled out a chair. Sawyer joined him.

Warren folded his hands on the tabletop. "This visit is regarding unfortunate news." He held Sawyer's gaze.

Sawyer leaned back and nodded.

"It's about your aunt Wanda's will—"

Sawyer jumped up, heart in his throat. "What's happened? Is she okay?"

Warren's eyes widened, then he blinked. "She's fine. Please sit down."

Sawyer returned to the chair but sat on the edge, trying to calm his breathing.

"I mean, she's as well as expected under the

circumstances."

Sawyer narrowed his eyes. "What circumstances?"

"The cancer, of course." Warren frowned.

"Cancer? Oh hell," Sawyer uttered, rubbing his chin.

"You didn't know?" Warren tapped the tabletop with a manicured finger.

"No. I knew she'd gone to the doctor a few times, but she wouldn't say more than that." Sawyer squeezed his eyes shut. It felt as if a rock landed on his chest. He scrubbed his face.

His eccentric old aunt had never married. She was his last living relative on the Hickey side of the family.

The last time he'd seen her had been at church. She'd scanned him from head to boots before her crony, Desire Hardmann, had grabbed Wanda's elbow and whisked her to a group of ladies planning a bake sale.

He regretted not speaking with her. Now that he thought about it, Sawyer hadn't seen her at church in a few weeks. He rubbed his stomach, trying to relieve the dread pooling there.

CHAPTER THREE

Stephanie

NAN O'WRIMO OPENED THE DOOR of the Cummings' manor. The older woman's bright-white smile contrasted her creamy milk chocolate skin. "Welcome, Stephanie. We'll be meeting upstairs today in Wanda's sitting room."

"I'm glad she's up to the historical society's meeting," Stephanie said, entering the foyer.

"Go on up. It's to the right. Second door on the left." Nan pointed.

Holding the thick handrail, Stephanie climbed but hesitated at the split. She continued up the left side and followed the hallway to the balcony overlooking the library.

Covered with heavy curtains, the windows let minimal light into the cavernous room. Sheets had been thrown over the leather chairs. It reminded her of something from a horror movie and was nothing like the brilliant room she'd seen before.

Only once before.

When Sawyer had lured her with the treasure. He'd caught her, then kissed her. She touched her lips and shivered, remembering his kiss. Breathless, she backed out of the library and hurried to the stairs.

Sandy Beach was huffing up the stairwell and met her eyes. "I thought it was to the right?"

"It is." Stephanie followed the realtor to the sitting room. Glancing around, Stephanie noted most of the committee had arrived.

Wanda sat in a small plush armchair, her walker within reach. She seemed frail despite her smile. She wore a pink short-sleeved blouse, exposing several gauze pads taped to her arms.

Stephanie nodded to the other women and Walter Mellon. She found a seat on a mauve camelback sofa. Nan came in with a pitcher of lemonade and began pouring glasses. Sandy helped pass them out.

"Thank y'all for coming here," Wanda said, sweeping her arm in a grand gesture.

"No problem," Sandy said. "We're just glad you're up to it."

"Yes," Walter agreed.

"So, what about 155 Main Street?" Wanda asked, glancing at a paper. "Are they complying with the historical district yet?"

Walter cleared his throat. "I spoke with the owner. They plan to get quotes on the restoration."

"Good," Wanda said, relaxing against the back of her chair.

As the meeting continued, Stephanie watched Wanda. Her shoulders drooped, and the older woman hid a few yawns.

Stephanie met Nan's gaze. She shook her head and pursed her lips. Nan and Wanda had been friends most of their adult life, both never married or had children. Stephanie had heard some of their adventures of traveling together.

After the meeting ended, Stephanie helped Nan take the glasses to the kitchen. Nan washed the pitcher.

"Wanda would like to speak with you if you can spare a few moments," Nan said as she dried the pitcher.

"Sure, if you think she's up to it," Stephanie replied. "I don't want to wear her out."

Nan sighed and faced Stephanie. "I'm worried about her. Her energy isn't what it used to be. She naps all the time. I'm glad she has this group and so many friends who visit. It keeps her mind occupied."

"So, should I leave then?" Stephanie chewed her lip.

"Heavens no, child." Nan chuckled; her eyes crinkled into half-moons. "You march up there and talk to her or else I'll never hear the end of it."

Stephanie nodded. "I'll save you."

"Shoo. Better go or Wanda will come find you." Nan waved the dishtowel.

Once Stephanie had reached the door, Nan called, "I like her idea. I hope you will too."

Curiosity had Stephanie dashing up the stairs. Breathing deeply, she calmed her racing heart. *Another mystery at the Cummings' estate.*

Wanda glanced up with inviting blue eyes. "Thanks for coming, Stephanie. I know you probably have plans."

"You're my date tonight, Ms. Hickey," Stephanie said, taking the vacant seat next to Wanda.

"That's surprising for a pretty young lady." Wanda patted Stephanie's arm. "I have a question for you. Is it true you're looking for a place to live?"

Stephanie nodded. "Yes. My landlord sold the building, and I have to move out by the end of the month."

"I have a proposition for you..." Wanda stood with the

support of her walker. "Come over to the window, dear. See the garage? It has an apartment. Would you like to live on the Cummings' Estate?"

Stephanie stared at the four-car garage with the full second story. The property was further from town and the bank, but the countryside was beautiful. She squelched her excitement to ask, "How much is the rent?"

"The first month is free, but I'm sure it won't be more than you're paying now. It's been empty for years, and it needs the cleaning of the century." Wanda tapped the window glass. "It will be nice to have a neighbor. I'd love to chitchat more about the town. Nan's circle is limited." She tittered, then began coughing.

Nan rushed in with a worried expression. "Come rest." She pointed to Wanda's chair.

Wanda nodded and eased over and relaxed down with a sigh. She sipped water from the cup Nan handed her.

"Well?" Nan asked Stephanie.

"It's a generous offer. Thank you. I'll take it." Stephanie moved to the window and inspected the building again.

Nan and Wanda glanced at each other with wide grins. "Why don't you go visit the apartment and see if you like it." Nan handed Wanda her large beige purse from the table. Wanda rummaged around, plucking out a keyring. She selected a key with green glittery nail polish painted on it and dangled it. "Here's the key."

With a gleaming smile and key in hand, Stephanie went to explore her new home.

CHAPTER FOUR

Sawyer

Sawyer stood, finger poised over the doorbell, and inhaled. It wasn't as if he'd never heard a will read. It had been four years since his father, Seymour, had passed. He glanced over his shoulder at the unkempt yard. The birds tried to bathe in what little water remained in the fountain.

Since Sawyer's mother had run off with another man, it had been Sawyer's dad, aunt, and him on the Cummings' Estate. Then his dad passed. Sawyer had used his inheritance to party his grief and loneliness away. Money couldn't buy love or happiness. It took a steady, hard job to mature him. Sawyer scrubbed his face; perhaps he shouldn't have ever left.

After the lawyer had delivered the news, Sawyer had noticed the townsfolk slyly glancing at him, then murmuring with heads together. He speculated the seriousness of his aunt's condition had circulated.

He surveyed the large double door once more. With faded and peeling paint, the home was past its prime, just like its resident.

Nan answered the door. "What are you doing ringing the

bell?" She put her hands on her hips and frowned.

"I, uh—" Sawyer stuttered, rubbing his head.

"I'm just playing with you. Come in, honey. She'll be glad to see you." Nan opened the door and embraced him.

"Is she feeling up to this?" Sawyer asked, trying to mask his worried tone.

"She's tired, but expecting you. She'd be disappointed if you didn't visit with her."

Sawyer nodded, then took the steps two at a time to the top. He hurried toward his aunt's suite. Her door yawned open. The curtains were drawn, casting strange shadows. She reclined in a lounge chair, a scarf around her head, her eyes closed and a blanket over her lap. Sawyer held his breath, observing her pale face. The blanket moved as she stirred. Her lids flickered open, and she smiled.

"There's my favorite nephew." Wanda lifted a hand. He took it and squeezed gently.

"I'm your only nephew. I've missed you, Auntie." He stooped and kissed her soft cheek.

She motioned to the armchair beside her.

"How's the ranch?" Wanda asked without giving him a chance to inquire about her health. He jumped into a story about Gimme Malone's dirty dancing routine.

Warren Teed knocked on the doorjamb. "Nan has instructed me to keep our meeting short." He set his briefcase on a small coffee table and sat on the sofa, then opened the briefcase, shuffling some folders around.

"Oh, fiddlesticks. Nan is not my nursemaid," Wanda remarked, waving her hand.

"No, but she is a good friend," Warren responded. "Only good friends get to boss your guests around."

Wanda chuckled, then nodded. "Nan has been a trouper. I

hope one day I can repay the favor…" She glanced toward the window and frowned. Wanda pressed her lips together, then shook her head. "About my will…"

Sawyer inhaled sharply. Staring at his hands, he didn't grasp Warren's reply. "What did you say?"

Warren blinked and scanned Wanda before repeating, "We are waiting on another party before we start."

"Someone else is coming to the will reading?" Sawyer asked.

A brunette slid into the room, her hair cascading over her face. "Sorry, I'm late. Nan handed me the mail and—"

"Do you still have two ears? That woman can talk your ear off," Wanda chuckled.

The woman brushed her hair away from her face.

Sawyer stood. "Stephanie." She met his gaze, a slight blush fanning her cheeks as she nodded. He waited until she took a seat beside Warren before he returned to his chair.

"Now that we are all here, we can start." Warren nodded to Wanda.

Wanda took a sip of water. "I want to say thank you for coming. Sawyer, I know that ranch you work for has you slaving away at all hours, so I appreciate your time."

"Of course, Auntie." He held her hand again.

Warren cleared his throat and began reading. It was the usual legal speak reminding Sawyer of Seymour's estate, including finances. Sawyer had no knowledge of his aunt's net worth, but honestly, he didn't need her money. His father's estate was adequate to sustain him.

"This list of items will belong to Mr. Sawyer Hickey if he follows these two stipulations."

Sawyer stared at his boots. Wanda squeezed his hand. "Don't worry."

Warren peered over his reading glasses. "One—Mr. Hickey must marry in order to receive the Cummings' manor house and the acreage surrounding it. Two—Miss Malone will be allowed to live on the premises until Sawyer marries or she decides to move out."

Sawyer glanced up and met Stephanie's gaze. "What the hell?" he mouthed. Stephanie shrugged, blushing again.

Nan came in carrying a glass and pill case. "Time for your medicine and a rest."

Wanda yawned, then tried to stand. The fuzzy peach blanket fell to her stocking feet, and stooping for it, she swiveled off balance. Sawyer caught her elbow and helped her into the bedroom. Stephanie brought the blanket and laid it on the foot of the bed.

"Good night, Aunt Wanda," Sawyer said, then kissed her cheek.

Nan waved them out of the room. "Goodnight, y'all."

Warren handed them each a packet, then closed his briefcase. "My card is stapled to the top. Call if you have any questions or when you get engaged." Warren winked as Sawyer threw his hands into the air.

"Married! I can't believe her," Sawyer groused. "It can't be legal."

"It isn't," Stephanie hissed. She put a finger over her mouth and motioned to the hallway.

Sawyer followed her as she continued down to the kitchen. "Your aunt only wants what's best for you," Stephanie said, hugging herself.

"What's best for me?" Sawyer slammed a fist on the table. "I don't think so."

Stephanie's sad eyes turned hard. She jumped in front of him, poking him in the chest. "You listen to me, Mr. Hickey.

Your aunt is dying, and she doesn't want you to be alone. Can you think about someone other than yourself for once?"

Words left him as if he'd been sucker-punched in the gut. He rubbed his face. The sweet smell of coconut caught his attention and calmed him. "You're right."

Stephanie's eyes widened. "I am?"

He traced her face. She stepped back, bumping into the island.

Sawyer sighed. "I'm sorry, it's just..." He turned around and glanced out the window. "I just found out about the cancer and now this—stipulation." He shook his head.

"It's fine." She patted his arm. "It must be a shock."

"Would you care to go to Hammered? I need a beer and to talk this thing out," Sawyer said, throwing her a hopeful side-glance.

Stephanie had her bottom lip between her teeth. She sighed and finally mumbled, "I don't know."

"I'd really like to hear how the interesting caveat of Miss Malone living at the Cummings' house came about." Sawyer crossed his arms.

Stephanie blanched and sighed again. "Fine."

CHAPTER FIVE

Stephanie

STEPHANIE ENTERED HAMMERED AND SCANNED the tavern for Sawyer. From a booth, he raised a hand. She nodded, then glanced around the room. The long wood bar was filled with patrons, most she knew.

Her brother, Gimme, played pool with the Double D Ranch owner, Josiah Barnes. She tilted her head, letting her hair hide her face. Gimme had a problem with his mouth; he didn't know when to shut it. The last thing she needed was for Gimme to blast his lone speculations to the restaurant.

In a tight skirt and low-cut top, Mona Little eagerly complimented the men who played pool. Mona worked under Stephanie at the bank as a teller. The sassy girl had a curvy figure men seemed to respond to, not to mention she offered kisses for the winners of the pool games. And Sawyer was particularly good at pool.

"What's wrong?" Sawyer asked as Stephanie slid into the booth.

"Well, I might have thought of a way out of the marriage thing." Stephanie watched as Mona recognized Sawyer sitting with Stephanie.

"What? That was fast." Sawyer grinned and relaxed back. "Are you this fast when it comes to making loans?"

Stephanie laughed. "Most of the time, yes."

"Wow." His gaze roamed her face. The room heated.

They ordered and once Sawyer fingered the neck of his green bottle, he said, "So, about your living situation…"

Stephanie glanced at her brother. "I moved into the house a week ago."

"Go on," he prompted, leaning over the table studying her.

"I'm part of the Fortuna Historical Society. We are responsible for the historical district and staffing the museum—"

"I know." Sawyer waved his hand. "My aunt loves that group."

"Yes. That's how it happened."

"How what happened?" Sawyer's eyes narrowed.

"My living arrangement," Stephanie responded. She took a sip of beer. "Wanda held a meeting in her suite and afterwards she asked me if I wanted to live in the apartment over the garage." She shrugged.

Sawyer tilted his head, then nodded. "I suppose Nan agreed it was a good idea to have someone on the premises with my aunt being sick."

"Wanda knows I love the house and want to get it declared a state treasure," Stephanie said.

"Treasure." Sawyer rolled his eyes.

Stephanie smirked. "Not that treasure. A real one. It's a historical landmark. One of the original Fortuna buildings."

"Hey, Hickey, you up for a game?" Josiah said as he passed with a pitcher of beer and a couple of empty mugs.

"Nah. Another time," Sawyer answered.

"It's better that way. I'm on a roll and would kick your butt." Josiah laughed at Sawyer's sour expression.

"If you'd like to play, don't let me stop you." Stephanie signaled Pixie Dix to bring another round.

Sawyer finished his bottle. "I'm good."

Mona turned her back on their table and Stephanie leaned forward. "You know, maybe you should play a game to get Mona in your good graces. It looks as if she isn't happy you're not playing."

Sawyer frowned and crossed his arms. "Listen, I'm not dating her. I've tried to distance myself from her and her..." his lips puckered as if he tasted a lemon, "clinginess."

"Clinginess? I thought you liked the attention. I've seen you two, the entire town has seen you two, after you win a game."

Sawyer cringed, then shrugged. "I used to like the attention. But she doesn't do a thing for me. We've never hooked up."

"That's not what Gimme says," Stephanie informed.

Sawyer's brows dipped as he turned red. "What did Gimme say?"

"What doesn't Gimme say? Gimme says a lot of crap, but it goes in one ear and out the other," Stephanie admitted, glancing at her brother who high-fived Mona.

"You too, huh?" Sawyer watched the pool players.

Stephanie snorted and covered her face as she giggled. Sawyer caught her laughter. She wiped her eyes and inhaled a deep breath.

Pixie delivered their beers. Stephanie lifted the bottle to her lips and almost choked when she caught Sawyer's sultry expression studying her mouth. She set the bottle on the table.

"About the will... I have an idea about the illegal part," Stephanie declared.

"I'm listening," Sawyer replied, folding his hands around the beer.

"Just appease Wanda. Get engaged. That will make Wanda happy and you can end it after Wanda... you know." Stephanie glanced into her lap.

"A pretend fiancée, huh?" Sawyer rubbed his chin. He stared off a few moments before focusing on Stephanie once more.

"Wanda can't make you get married, but if she thinks you're engaged, then maybe she'll be at peace. And then the will won't be held in probate." Stephanie hurried on, "I know it's a crazy idea, but Wanda is wonderful. She wants what's best for you. She gushes about you all the time." Stephanie felt her cheeks heat and looked away.

"I'd have to pick someone who'd be willing to go along with the ruse," he mused. "Wanda is smart. It can't be just any girl."

"You'd have to make it believable," Stephanie acknowledged.

"We'd announce the engagement, something public, and visit Wanda with the news," he said, knitting his brows. "But she wouldn't necessarily believe I'd found someone so soon."

"Can you move back to the Cummings' manor?" Stephanie asked. "Then your aunt would see you interacting more often."

"You want me to live with you?" Sawyer cracked a grin. "I suppose. I've already talked to my boss. He knows I'll be cutting my hours to help my aunt. It might be better if I quit. The house could use a little TLC."

Stephanie smiled and nodded, happy for Wanda.

"Now to select my fiancée?" Sawyer glanced around the building.

"How about Mona? She likes you," Stephanie suggested,

surprised and elated by Sawyer's grimace.

"How about one of the Hopkins' girls?" she suggested.

Sawyer shook his head and frowned. "Too young."

Stephanie sighed, trying to think of single women who could pull off the ruse while being kind to Wanda.

"It should be someone my aunt knows I have chemistry with."

"That would be helpful," Stephanie agreed.

"What size ring do you wear?" Sawyer asked, then took a drink.

"What? Why?" She gasped. "Oh no, no, no."

"Why not?" Sawyer pressed back against the booth, studying her face.

Words failed her, and she shook her head.

Sawyer slapped his palms on the table. "We've got history. She caught us—"

"I know she caught us. Thank God. Who knows what would have happened?" Under the table, Stephanie rubbed her hands together.

"We both know what would have happened if she hadn't interrupted us," Sawyer said, grinning. He winked.

The room became too hot, and Stephanie chugged her beer. She closed her eyes, but the memory of his lips on her neck had her heart rate rising.

"Come on, Steph," Sawyer pleaded. "Help me grant my aunt's wish."

She pursed her lips. The last thing she needed was a fake relationship.

He laid his hand on the table, palm up before her. Studying his calloused, ranch-worked hands, her heart grew giddy. He'd changed from that careless, ne'er-do-well rich kid to a hardworking man.

"If we do this…" she bit her lip.

"Don't worry. I won't hold you to it, and when the time comes, I'll release you. I'll take care of everything." He ran his fingers through his thick, dark hair.

Stephanie swallowed and rubbed her palms on her jeans. "Are you sure you don't want Mona?"

"Ah, heck no." He leaned over the table and narrowed his hungry eyes. "I want you, darlin'."

Suddenly the room lacked oxygen. Stephanie stood, clutching her purse against her. "I'll think about it." She strode out of the restaurant to her car.

Sitting in the stillness, she tried to calm her racing heart. Stephanie whispered into the darkness, "What have I done?"

CHAPTER SIX

Sawyer

SAWYER EXITED HIS TRUCK AND walked toward the florist. They had his aunt's favorite orchid in stock, and he planned to pick it up before he returned home. However, a jewelry store caught his attention. The dazzling photo of a diamond solitaire in the window lured him to the door. The bell rang when he entered Family Jewels.

"How may I assist you today?" asked a slender blonde woman with Jean Poole on her name badge.

"I'm interested in engagement rings," Sawyer replied.

"Congratulations," she said, motioning him to a glass case.

Sawyer swallowed, ogling the rings. "There are so many."

"Does your fiancée wear a lot of jewelry? Does she like gold, platinum, or titanium?" Jean smiled.

Sawyer rubbed his face. "She's not flashy and wears minimal accessories. I'm not sure which metal she'd prefer." Pretending to be engaged was going to be hard to pull off. He had to get the ring right. It needed to encapsulate the uniqueness of their relationship.

He recalled the weight of her in his arms, her soft curves pressed against him, the spark of her luminous blue eyes, and her shapeliness in the bluebonnet dress.

"Do you have something blue?" Sawyer asked.

"Yes. We have a sapphire wrap, here." Jean pointed to the dark, glimmering stones. "Some bands have small diamonds and sapphires."

Sawyer nodded but studied the various rings. "Who knew it would be so daunting? There are so many choices."

"Take your time. Let me know if you have any questions," Jean said, moving away from the case. The doorbell rang. Jean greeted another customer.

"Excuse me," Sawyer asked, waving his hand to get her attention. "What about this one?" He pointed to the back corner. The ring had become partially hidden by the black velvet cloth in the case. Luckily, his height allowed him to see the silver edge.

"Oh, that's a nice ring." She unlocked the case and retrieved the ring. Lighter than a sapphire, the gemstone sparkled in the light. The band had a braided, almost Celtic design. "It's a blue diamond."

"Perfect. It's the color of bluebonnets." Sawyer's heart warmed, and his stomach fluttered.

"So it is." Jean smiled as Sawyer lifted it close and examined the artisanship.

"This is the one." He grinned.

After he finalized the paperwork, he visited the florist and picked up the orchid and a bouquet. Glancing at the time, he frowned.

He drove like a madman from Nockerville toward Fortuna and arrived just before noon. Fridays were the busiest for a bank. Flowers in hand, he exited the safety of his truck and entered the stale vestibule. Four tellers all had customers, and several people waited in line.

Sawyer edged toward Stephanie's office. Her door was open, but an older man sat in the stiff-backed chair with his elbows on his knees. The man glanced up, his brows rising when he glimpsed the flowers.

"I think you have a visitor, Ms. Malone," the man stated,

pointing to the door.

Careful to hide the flowers, Sawyer popped his head in and said, "Hiya. I need a minute when you have one. Take your time. I'll be out here."

Stephanie closed her mouth and nodded. "It will be a few minutes."

He waved and ducked out again, winking at the man, who chuckled. Sawyer lowered himself to an empty chair outside Stephanie's office. He laid the flowers on another.

With a sigh, he leaned back and critiqued the decor. "Dusty fake plants," he grumbled. The marble floor needed a good polish. The clients moved in and out as if the bank breathed.

Sawyer recognized the guy teller from school. He'd been few years younger than Sawyer. Of course, the other teller he knew was Mona. She jerked her head when she noticed him. Brushing her hair behind her ear, she studied him. Her gaze slid to the flower bunch. Mona's brows rose.

"Thanks for coming to see me today, Mr. Longfellow. If you have any questions, don't hesitate to call. My card is on the front of your folder. Welcome to the Fortuna Savings and Loan family." Stephanie shook the man's hand and watched him leave before turning to Sawyer.

"What can I do for you, Mr. Hickey?" Stephanie asked.

Sawyer smirked as he stood. He couldn't help it.

"Wait. Don't answer that." With hands on her hips, she examined him from boots to cowboy hat and a faint blush crept over her cheeks.

"I've got something for you." He scooped up the flowers and offered them to her.

Her bright blue eyes inspected the assortment of colors as she took them. Closing her eyes, she lifted the bouquet to her nose. "Thank you." Once more she scrutinized him, her gaze stopping on his lips.

Sawyer swallowed. He fished inside his front pocket, silently cursing the tight denim. Small velvet box in hand, he dropped to one knee and lifted it.

Stephanie gasped and covered her mouth with her hands. Hushed voices murmured around them, but Sawyer couldn't steal his gaze away from Stephanie's glittering eyes.

Sawyer opened the lid, and Stephanie gasped again.

"It's beautiful." Her voice barely audible, she said, "It doesn't look fake."

"Remember the party? This is the same color as your dress, the shade of bluebonnets." His gaze dropped to the box. "Every time I see bluebonnets, I think of you in that dress." He met her gaze.

Stephanie stepped closer and caressed his face. "Really?"

Not trusting his voice, he nodded.

"Oh, Sawyer, it's perfect. I love bluebonnets."

"Ask her!" a teller hollered.

The atmosphere had gone, and he struggled to breathe. Sawyer wiped his brow. "I… I."

Stephanie's lips bowed into a grin and one delicate eyebrow rose.

Sawyer cleared his throat. "Will you marry me?"

Her gaze bore into his soul. Something merged and melted, becoming inseparable.

Her shining eyes filled. She nodded once and extended her left hand. Sawyer slid the ring onto her finger, then stood.

Hoots, hollers, and whistles filled the room as the onlookers cheered. Several people held their phones, capturing the proposal.

"Oh my…" The words gurgled out of Stephanie's mouth, her face turning fire engine red.

"Come here," Sawyer said, opening his arms. Stephanie fell in, burying her face against his chest and crushing the flowers. It had been years since he'd held her, but his body still reacted.

The scent of coconut swirled around, tingling his senses. He tipped her head backward and gazed into those luminous blue pools. He lowered his lips to hers. A sweet, gentle kiss that had the audience ahhhing.

Sawyer broke the kiss, but she focused on his lips. His heart kicked up a gear, and he dove in again, this time with pent-up longing.

Stephanie moaned and snaked her hands around his back, her touch igniting his skin.

The audience clapped and continued to make noise. "This is going on Facebook," a woman said.

Stephanie groaned and pulled away. She hit his chest. "I could kill you," she hissed, hurrying to her office.

"Congratulations on your engagement," the male teller called. "When are you getting married?"

"Whoa," Sawyer replied. "One thing at a time." He laughed nervously, then entered Stephanie's office and closed the door.

Sawyer began to pace the cramped space. He'd done it. They'd become engaged very publicly. He knew the display would fuel the gossipmongers. Nothing's juicier in a small town than fresh gossip, except maybe extra-rare prime rib.

"You should be happy," Stephanie said dryly. She'd returned to her desk and appeared tired, rubbing her cheek, her posture like a wilted leaf.

Sawyer sensed something was wrong. He eased into the stiff-backed chair. "I'll be happy if you like the ring."

The weariness of her face eased some, and a smile flickered over her lips. "It's beautiful."

"Like you," he said, rising. He rounded the desk and once more pulled her into his arms. "What I said about the ring was true. It reminds me of you, that's why I got it."

She nodded against his chest. "I love it."

"Sorry about the spur-of-the-moment proposal, but with all the witnesses, my aunt can't doubt it, can she? Especially with one of her church lady friends as a witness." Sawyer squeezed her gently.

"We'll see."

CHAPTER SEVEN

Stephanie

STEPHANIE CARRIED A BAG OF groceries toward her apartment, nodding at Sawyer as he and a contractor stood facing the house. Sawyer had a list of improvements about the length of his arm.

She put the ice cream in the freezer and turned to get the other bags when Sawyer stalked inside, bringing the rest.

"You didn't have to do that, but thanks," she said.

"No problem." He set the groceries on the table and kissed her cheek, then swirled around in a circle. "Wow. This place looks great. I love the gray walls."

Stephanie continued to put away the items as he commented on her choice of decor. After his fifth remark, she narrowed her eyes. "What's with your sudden interest in the decor?"

Sawyer sheepishly leaned against the cabinets. "Am I that obvious?" He laughed.

She crossed her arms and tapped her foot.

"Okay. My aunt wants you to join us for lunch after church," Sawyer said with a smirk.

"Oh," Stephanie squeaked.

"Don't worry. I don't bite. Well, not usually. And Nan will be there too." Sawyer stuck his hands in his front pockets. "I hope that's okay."

"Yeah, sure." Stephanie blinked. Sawyer had disappeared.

Good grief. Her heart always worked double time when Sawyer came near. She glanced at the ring and her stomach fluttered.

A car honked. Stephanie peered out the window, down onto the driveway. Her brother's little beater sedan had parked next to her car.

Sawyer faced away from the apartment, and she admired his shorts clinging against his backside. He had inches over Gimme, but in the last year her younger brother had filled out. His voice had deepened and his brow and beard had become heavier. *Now if he'd only learn when to keep his mouth shut.* He spoke, waving his arms. She giggled. "Typical Gimme."

Stephanie decided to rescue Sawyer. She scurried down the stairs and out into the balmy afternoon.

"Gimme, what are you doing here?" Stephanie called.

When the men turned, both had balled fists and crimson faces. *Oh, no.* "What's happening here?" she asked. Her gaze slid to Sawyer, and his eyes softened.

"What the hell, Steph?" Gimme said, finding his voice. "Why him and why didn't you tell the family?"

"Which question do you want answered first?" She canted her head, earning a chuckle from Sawyer. Gimme resembled a red chili pepper.

"We're engaged. Get over it." Hands on her hips, Stephanie glanced up at Wanda's window. The older woman regarded the scene intently.

"I won't see my sister married to this clown," Gimme

hissed.

"I'm sorry I didn't call you and let you know," Stephanie said, sliding to Sawyer's side. "It was sudden, and I needed time to soak it in."

Sawyer put his arm over her shoulder and she slid hers around his waist. "Are you going to be okay? I need to talk to the contractor before he leaves."

"I'm fine," Stephanie said.

"Good." Sawyer kissed her cheek, and she sighed, watching him go. She wanted to confide in her brother about the farce, but she knew better. That juicy tidbit would slip through his non- filter in a matter of minutes, first to her sisters, parents, then the ranch hands.

Stephanie faced her brother, taking his calloused hands. "Please be happy for me." She giggled. "I'm engaged."

Gimme's color faded to pink, and he nodded. "I'll try, but the whole town knows. Mom found out while getting her hair done. She saw it on someone's phone."

Stephanie covered her face. "Mom and Dad are going to kill me."

"Actually, Dad knew but didn't say a word about it. I suppose he didn't know when Sawyer was going to pop the question," Gimme said, kicking the ground. "Mom is mad at Dad."

"Wait. Sawyer asked Dad for my hand? Wow." Stephanie's heart lodged in her throat, and she swallowed. "I can't believe he talked to him."

"I guess it's the real deal," Gimme said, touching her arm. He sighed. "Congratulations."

"Thank you." Stephanie pointed to the garage. "Come see my apartment."

"Did you find the treasure yet?" Gimme asked like an

excited puppy waiting for a treat.

"No, but there's a vintage Porsche in the garage. It was Sawyer's dad's. Do you want to see it?

"Is a frog's ass watertight?"

"Come on then." As she led her brother away, she glanced toward her fiancé, and caught him watching her. Her stomach fluttered again, but she smiled.

CHAPTER EIGHT

Sawyer

SAWYER FELL INTO A ROUTINE. He worked with contractors making the manor house more accessible for his aunt. He ticked house prep, priming, and painting off the list. He'd bought shrubbery and planned to landscape around the manor. The roofers had been scheduled. He'd contacted the Double D and Big Deal ranches to negotiate the purchase of stock.

He planned to breed longhorns, but first he needed a barn or two and a fence. The Cummings' Estate had a crazy amount of acreage he wanted to put to use.

While Stephanie worked at the bank, she'd often have dinner with him and Wanda. Sawyer would take Stephanie by the hand and walk the property or gardens, and sometimes, if his aunt felt up to it, they'd all relax on the porch, watching the sunset.

The more sunsets he spent with Stephanie, the more comfortable he grew. He savored the moments studying her expression of awe as the hues morphed from brilliant red and golds to muted purples and pink, and he treasured the time with his aunt.

In four weeks' time, Sawyer and Stephanie's relationship had been accepted. Even Gimme boasted about his sister living on the Cummings estate.

Seemingly bolstered by the engagement, Wanda had returned to her usual spot in the front church pew. Sawyer took Stephanie's hand during prayer, and afterward she didn't pull away. Her coconut scent reminded him of summer.

It came as no surprise to Sawyer when Wanda invited a bunch of her first-pew friends for lunch at the manor. "I heard rumors we get to sample the Cummings' famous chocolate gravy," Desire said to Sawyer.

"I can't tell you," he replied, nodding to Stephanie's parents as they passed him. They met her at the end of the aisle. Stephanie's floral dress hugged her curves, and Sawyer swallowed.

"If he tells you the secret, then he'll have to kill you," Nan said, linking elbows with Desire.

"That's a shame. I can think of other things he could do to me instead," Desire lamented.

Sawyer's gaze jerked back to the older women. Desire's eyes sparkled with unbridled mischief while Nan covered her face with her hands. He hesitated before leaving to find Stephanie.

"Steph, looks like we're hosting an invasion of blue-hairs today." Sawyer thumbed over his shoulder to the posse of first pew ladies amassing in the center aisle.

She giggled. "Are you wanting to go, so we strategize our counter maneuvers?" She cocked her hip, causing her shirt to sway. In open-toed sandals, her blue toenails caught his attention. His gaze flowed upward from her ankles to her shapely calves.

He blinked and nodded.

Once at the homestead, Stephanie hopped out of the car. "I'm going to change really quick." She scuttled out of sight.

"I don't have that luxury," Sawyer mumbled, making his way to the kitchen. He rolled up his shirtsleeves and mixed the batter for biscuits.

Stephanie snuck into the kitchen and hugged him. He nearly dropped the bowl. "Watch it." He turned, catching a glimpse of her new ensemble of a pale blue short-sleeve shirt and khaki shorts.

"I'll set the table." She whisked out of the room with a handful of utensils.

Wanda's guests arrived, and Sawyer and Stephanie brought them coffee and juice. The older women chattered and cackled while he and Stephanie worked together like pros.

Wanda's cronies enjoyed their menu of homemade biscuits with their choice of chocolate or sausage gravy and fruit salad. The chocolate gravy had been passed down through the generations of his family. He treasured it more than any fictionalized cache of booty.

"Your future niece-in-law is a hard worker," Rose Bush gushed.

"Yes," Lily White agreed. "And she's such a pretty little thing."

"Has she toned down Sawyer's wild ways?" Missy Terchance asked.

"I hope, for her sake, not too much," Desire Hardmann said, wiggling her brows at Sawyer as he refilled her juice then removed empty dishes from the table.

Sawyer chuckled and hoped Stephanie couldn't make out the conversation from the kitchen. He brought the dirty plates to the counter. She stared at the engagement ring as the coffee pot filled. The shade of her shirt enhanced the blue diamond, making the color surreal. Her lips tipped in a smile, and his heart raced.

When she noticed his presence, she dropped her hand, and she blushed. "I think having the girls over has been good for your aunt. Their energy—"

"And all the gossip," Sawyer added.

Stephanie giggled, her button-nose crinkling, and Sawyer fought an urge to kiss it.

"That too. She loves hearing about their kids and grandkids, though." Stephanie picked up the carafe but paused at the doorway. "We've given her something that's strictly hers to brag about." She winked, pushing the door open with her bottom.

Sawyer rubbed his face, the warmth in his chest fascinating him.

Many of the ladies left, but Nan and Desire lingered, sitting on the back patio with Wanda. Sawyer excused himself and changed into work clothes. Sunshiny weather with a breeze afforded him the chance to work on the landscaping. He chose to plant some shrubs near the patio where the women relaxed.

He plunged his spade into the soil and scooped out the dirt. The afternoon sun beat down on him. Sweat broke out and trickled down his back. There'd been a time when he wouldn't have thought hard work was satisfying, but not anymore. He enjoyed working until he ached.

Stephanie sat beside his aunt and patted her hand. The tender scene tugged at his heartstrings even while guilt about lying nagged at him.

Desire and Nan leaned with their heads together. "Well, tell him," Nan said, elbowing Desire.

"Fine. Hey, Sawyer, you look hot. Why don't you take off your shirt?" Desire goaded.

Blushing, Stephanie laughed while his aunt shook her head.

"Great idea," Sawyer hollered back. He made a show of lifting his shirt, keeping his gaze locked on Stephanie's face. Her gaze remained glued to his torso, making every bead of perspiration feel like gas for a flame. He lifted the material over his head, then dropped it at his feet. He grinned at Stephanie, whose mouth had fallen open. She swallowed, then smiled.

"Woo-hoo! Now your jeans!" Desire yelled, clapping.

Sawyer returned his attention to the plant, dropping the root ball into the hole. He glanced up, sensing a commotion.

Nan stood with a wave. "I'll find it."

"No. You sit and enjoy your visit. I'll get it." Stephanie rose. He appreciated how her shirt and shorts accented her femininity. She disappeared into the house. His aunt wore the little smirk that said she'd gotten her way.

Sawyer moved on to the next hole. Halfway done, Stephanie appeared at his side.

"I'm sorry to interrupt your work—"

"Any excuse to stop will do. Especially when a beautiful lady does the stopping." He leaned against the shovel handle.

She shifted her weight as the pretty blush returned. "So, do you want thirty or fifty SPF sunscreen?"

Sawyer's gaze dropped to her hands. She held a tube of lotion and a spray can. She shook the sunscreen. "Ticktock. You're getting sunburned while you decide."

"I don't need it," he said, shaking his head.

Items still in her hands, she put her hands on her hips. "You will use it."

"Or what?" he grinned.

"I'll tell." She cocked her head to the side, and a sly grin slid onto her lips.

"Go ahead. I dare you." He leaned into her space, but she didn't back away.

"Aunt Wanda, Sawyer won't use the sunscreen," Stephanie tattled.

Wanda jumped up, giving Nan and Desire a scare. She moved as fast as her spindly legs could carry her with her friends close behind.

Sawyer closed his mouth as his aunt approached. She

pointed at him. "You put that sunscreen on right now, young man. You need to protect your skin from the sun. I don't want you getting skin cancer. It's not fun."

"Your skin is your biggest organ," Nan stated.

"Maybe not," Desire said, glancing at Sawyer's pants.

Stephanie lifted the choices again.

"I'll rub the lotion on him." Desire edged closer, rubbing her hands together.

"No, that's okay. Steph can do it. Can't you, darlin'?" Sawyer grinned at her wide eyes and open mouth.

Stephanie handed the spray back to Wanda, then picked up his T-shirt, shaking off the debris. "Turn around."

She wiped his back, then squirted some lotion into her hands. The cool sunscreen and her warm hands sliding over his skin relaxed his aching muscles. She massaged it into his skin. "Here," she said when it came time to apply it to his chest.

He raised his dirty hands. "Would you mind?"

"I'll do it," Desire offered, raising a hand.

"Come on," Nan said, tugging Desire back toward the patio.

Stephanie wiped him dry again. How he wished he'd just popped out of the shower and she was toweling him off. He closed his eyes and hummed as her fingers skimmed his pecks. Opening his eyes, he found Stephanie studying him with yearning. He tipped her head and gazed into those deep blue orbs.

He lowered his lips to hers, and she gasped. She opened for him, and he swept in. She tasted sweet and fresh. Forgetting his dirty hands, he plunged them into her hair. The scent of summer swirled around, tantalizing him.

Her hands wrapped around his back and tightened.

They broke apart, breathless. "Your kiss is addicting," he mumbled, his forehead pressed to hers.

She smiled and sucked his bottom lip. He moaned, diving in again. His heart struggled to escape from his chest. He didn't need oxygen, he needed Stephanie.

CHAPTER NINE

Stephanie

ONE MONTH LATER...

Stephanie held her breath. Her heart always raced when she saw Sawyer. Not only then, but thinking about the handsome devil made it pitter-patter too. She should have distanced herself from him, but it was late to guard her heart.

She'd been foolish to allow the pretend engagement because she'd fallen for Sawyer—hard.

What would happen when Wanda was gone? Would Sawyer want Stephanie like she wanted him? She shook her head.

"Are you ready to go?" Stephanie asked Wanda, taking her hand to help her down the front steps.

"Ready and willing." Wanda shifted her bowling-bag-like purse. "I'll treat to ice cream after the appointment."

"Sounds great." Stephanie drove toward Fortuna. Wanda had an oncology appointment. Ice cream was nice, but a couple of beers or a few shots would be more appropriate if she received bad news.

In the waiting room, Stephanie tried not to think sad thoughts. Wanda cheerfully chatted with the receptionist, whom she knew by name.

Stephanie pretended to read a decorating magazine. Her stomach churned. She was a liar. Her life with Sawyer, a hoax. Wanda deserved to know the truth, and Stephanie couldn't live with the falsehood any longer. It hurt.

She walked with Wanda and the nurse to the private room. The nurse asked questions and took Wanda's blood pressure.

"This is my soon-to-be niece," Wanda said with a bright smile.

Stephanie sunk back into the orange plastic chair and wiped damp palms on her pants. She'd breathe easier after she confessed.

"My nephew had to meet the plumber or he would have brought me. He's fixing up my house."

"That's great you have family close," the nurse said, smiling.

"He's a good boy," Wanda boasted. "Someday, I'll be a great-aunt." Stephanie closed her eyes, biting her lip.

The nurse smiled. "The doctor will be in shortly. He's finishing up with another patient."

The door clicked shut, filling the awkward silence. Stephanie jumped up and paced the small space. Wanda watched, her brow lowering a small bit with each pass.

"What's wrong?" Wanda asked, crossing her ankles and tilting her head.

"I need to tell you something." Stephanie rubbed her hands and stopped with the door behind her.

"Are you pregnant?" Wanda asked.

"No." Stephanie glanced at the floor, blinking her eyes refusing to cry. "It's not like that."

Something brushed the door, but it didn't open. Stephanie moved a few steps closer to the table.

"It's about Sawyer and me. We aren't really engaged. We pretended... to make you happy." She swallowed. The door made the weird noise again, but she ignored it. "You were really sick, and he wanted to give you peace. He didn't want you to think he'd be alone."

Wide-eyed, Wanda cleared her throat. "Y'all seemed so in love. I would have never known it to be anything but the truth." She glanced around the room, then focused behind Stephanie.

Stephanie lowered her head again. "That's because it is the truth, at least for my part. I'm falling for Sawyer, and that's why I had to tell you. I have to end it. It's too hard to live with it when it will be nothing more than a lie." She wiped her eyes.

A hand landed on her shoulder, and Stephanie jumped. She twirled around into a man's embrace. Recognizing his scent—fresh linen mixed with his spicy cologne—she inhaled. His warmth and arms soothed her.

Her eyes snapped open. What had he heard? She pushed back, her face on fire. She scanned his face. He wore a wolfish grin, making her long to kiss him. She swallowed.

"Do you mean it?" Sawyer asked, stroking her cheek.

"What did you hear?" she asked, glancing at Wanda, who held her hands as if she prayed.

Sawyer took Stephanie's hands in his and squeezed. "I heard you come clean to Auntie Wanda and the reason why."

"Oh," Stephanie met his eyes.

"Is it true?" Sawyer asked again, this time in a whisper.

Stephanie nodded, and he pulled her against him into a bear hug. He hadn't rejected her. Joy permeated her heart and tears escaped.

"Young man, you need to tell her." Wanda pointed at Sawyer.

"I know."

"Tell me what?" Stephanie asked, gazing into his hooded eyes.

"I..." Sawyer blushed and grinned a lopsided smile. "I... ugh."

"Oh, for Pete's sake, he loves you, too." Wanda stood with her hands on her hips. "Kids these days."

"Is it true?" Stephanie asked, hope taking flight in her soul.

"Oh, hell yeah," Sawyer replied, descending on her lips.

Fire lapped at her skin and worked its way in, filling her completely. She couldn't breathe, and she couldn't move other than to press closer.

"Stephanie." His breath feathered her neck, sending a shiver down her spine. "I can't get enough of you. Thinking about our engagement ending leaves me feeling empty. I need you, Steph."

Tears welled in her eyes, and she wiped them away as the doctor entered the office. Wanda gushed about her nephew and his fiancée as if no proclamations had ever happened.

"Kids, why don't you go to the waiting room," Wanda said. "I'll be out in a few minutes."

Sawyer and Stephanie waited, her head on his shoulder and their fingers laced, watching the minutes evaporate. "Do you think she'll have good news?" Stephanie dared to ask.

"I should have stayed and talked with the doctor," Sawyer admitted, squeezing Stephanie's hand.

"There she is." Stephanie pointed to the checkout area. "I'll go get my car and meet you at the door."

Sawyer nodded. He helped Wanda into the car and closed

the door. Stephanie didn't know how to ask about what the doctor had to say without sounding nosy. She didn't bring it up, and Wanda seemed quieter than usual.

Stephanie prayed that she was only tired and hadn't had dire news.

EPILOGUE

Stephanie

AT THE CUMMINGS' ESTATE, WANDA was out of the car and inside the house before Stephanie turned the ignition off. She met Sawyer at the door.

"Wanda didn't say two words the whole drive home," Stephanie said, holding his arm. "I hope she's okay."

He frowned. "Me too."

"Kids." Wanda leaned over the balcony down at them. "Come to my suite. We need to talk."

Sawyer and Stephanie glanced into each other's eyes and climbed the stairway together. Stephanie chewed on her bottom lip. They sat together on the sofa.

Wanda sighed. "It's my turn to confess."

Stephanie felt Sawyer tense, and she patted his leg.

Wanda stood straight and appeared less feeble. Her cheeks had a healthy flush, most likely from the hurried stair climb.

"I may have exaggerated my condition." Wanda glanced out the window.

"Condition?" Sawyer narrowed his eyes and leaned forward.

"My health. I led you to believe it's worse than it is."

"But the cancer—"

49

"I had melanoma and needed surgery to remove some spots. That's why I'm a stickler about sunscreen. If I would have taken better care of my skin, it's possible I wouldn't have had skin cancer."

"But the headscarf?" Stephanie asked.

"Rose bought it for me, so I had to wear it. It's lovely, but I didn't lose my hair."

"The will?" Sawyer growled.

"Part of the ruse. Nan told me you'd be furious with me, but…"

Stephanie put a hand on Sawyer's arm. "She wanted you to get serious about your future."

"Stephanie is right. I didn't want you to live life alone. I know what it's like, and I don't want that for you." Wanda shook her head. "Then I met Stephanie at the historical preservation meetings, and I remembered your tête-à-tête."

Stephanie chuckled nervously.

Wanda continued, "You've grown into a wonderful, kind woman. I knew you'd be perfect for my Sawyer."

"Auntie Wanda, I can't believe you." Sawyer crossed his arms.

"Hey, an aunt's got to do what an aunt's got to do if she wants to live long enough to see her great nieces or nephews."

Stephanie stood, hugging herself. "And the cancer?"

"I'm cancer free, but I have to go back for checkups. They are watching a few spots. The one spot on my leg they had to dig pretty deep to get it out. It hurt like the dickens when I walked, so that's why I used the walker." Wanda lifted her pants leg and exposed a taped gauze pad.

Stephanie hugged Wanda. "I'm so glad you're fine," Stephanie said, her voice gravelly with emotion.

"Damn. We would have had a really long engagement," Sawyer stated, waggling his finger at his aunt.

Wanda shrugged and laughed. "I've enjoyed having you both here."

"Well, we've all come clean today," Sawyer laughed.

"I feel better." Stephanie gazed into Sawyer's sultry eyes.

"I'm glad you know the truth, and you've found each other. Now, if we could only find the treasure." Wanda rubbed her chin, then turned toward her bedroom.

"I found my treasure," Sawyer said, pulling Stephanie into his arms.

"Not in here, young man," Wanda said, shaking her finger.

"Yes, ma'am." Sawyer took Stephanie by the hand and led her to the balcony overlooking the library.

"Are we looking for the treasure?" She studied the wall of books.

"It's not exactly what I had in mind," he said. His velvety, sensual tone had her heart racing.

She quirked a brow. "What—"

His lips descended to hers as he pressed her against the bookcase. Sawyer plunged his fingers into her long, ebony hair. She tugged at his shirt until she was free to skim his skin with her hands.

He moaned and lowered her to the ground. Wedged between the wall of books and the railing, she stared up as he sucked and nipped at her neck.

She wrapped her legs around his waist and squeezed. "Darlin', you don't know what you do to me," he breathed, fanning her neck.

Stephanie's unfocused gaze toured the ceiling, then slid to the colored book spines. She gasped.

Sawyer sat up, breathing heavily. "Are you hurt?"

"No." She blinked. "What did your father say about this room and the treasure?"

"Dad said this room is the key to the treasure."

"Are you sure he didn't say the key to the treasure is in this room?" she asked.

"It's the same. Why?"

"Because I think I found it." Stephanie kneeled before the bookcase, feeling the smooth hardwood underside of a low shelf. She bit her lip, finding a divot. "Ah ha! I had to slide the pocket back."

"Pocket?" Sawyer kneeled beside her, watching.

"Voila!" Stephanie held a black skeleton key, dangling it like bait.

"Holy hell." Sawyer gaped. He lowered himself to inspect the isolated cubby that had hidden the key. "I wonder what it opens?"

"My heart," she said, with a sly grin.

In an instant, he was on her once more, his firm body pressing her to the carpet. His caresses had every nerve tingling. As Sawyer loved her, Stephanie relaxed her arm, letting her hand fall between the balcony rails. She opened her fist. The key bobbled, falling to the first floor with a clang.

Sawyer gazed into her eyes and smirked. "No more pretending. You're my treasure, Steph. I don't need anything but you."

Love a book?

Please leave a review.

Reviews are like virtual hugs
for authors.

AVAILABLE

The Fortuna, Texas Series
★Fortuna Full Length Novels★
The Double D Ranch Book
Plumb Twisted
More Than a Fantasy
Municipal Liaisons

★Fortuna Novellas★
Here We Go Again
The Playboy's Pretend Fiancée
Cole's New Song

★The Fortuna Dare Society★
Brad
A Book Club for Men

★Other Books★
Dragonfly Wishes
Dragunzel
Pandemonium in Peoria
The Secret Shelf

Cole's New Song
Coming May 2023

A continuation of Cole and Piper's story from *Plumb Twisted*.

An exciting day spent celebrating his best friend's engagement is what Cole had planned, but after a worrisome appointment wedding themes are the last thing on his mind.

Piper suspects something is upsetting Cole. Helping her besties create custom lingerie and decorations for the naughty nuptials kills time until she's able to sit her man down for a heart to heart. Using her skills as a lingerie beta tester might pry the words free, and his pants, too.

Can they face what the future holds together, or will Cole face the music alone?

The Secret Shelf

I'm Kate, and I work in a dream store full of local artisans' wares and indie authors' books. At the Secret Shelf rumors fly and maybe a dragon or ghost or two. Okay, not dragons.

Besides helping someone find the perfect book—yes, I have read at least one from each author, my other jobs include, but are not limited to, coaxing the statuesque new girl away from the customer service desk, dodging my boss, sipping Blissful Beans, and crushing on Brody.

Brody—what can I say beyond yum? He could have stepped out of a skinny jean ad. Hair with highlights I'd paid for, manicured hands, smells like heaven, and has a tight—well, you get the idea.

Too bad he's gay

ABOUT THE AUTHOR

Rochelle puts an artistic spin on everything she does, but there are two things she fails at miserably:

1. Cooking (seriously, she can burn water)

2. Sewing (buttons immediately fall back off)

But she loves baking and makes a mean BTS (better than sex) cake.

When in observation mode she is quiet, however, her mouth is usually open with an encouraging glass-is-half-full pun or, quite possibly, her foot. She's a Bearcat, a Buckeye, an interior decorator, and fluent in sarcasm.

Every November Rochelle takes on the challenge of National Novel Writing Month (NaNoWriMo.org) where she endeavors to write 50,000 words in thirty days. You can often hear her cheering the Dayton area Wrimos (those who join her in this crazy pursuit).

She loves to connect with readers. You can find her on Facebook (search for Author Rochelle Bradley), TikTok, YouTube, Twitter, Pinterest, TikTok, Tumblr, and Instagram.

Visit Rochelle's website to sign up for her newsletter to keep up to date about future novels and book signings: RochelleBradley.com.

Made in the USA
Monee, IL
02 June 2023